Terrible, Terrible TIGER

Written and illustrated by

Colin and Jacqui Hawkins

WALKER BOOKS
AND SUBSIDIARIES
LONDON • BOSTON • SYDNEY

There once was a terrible tiger,
so terrible to see.

There once was a terrible tiger,
as fierce as fierce could be.

There once was a terrible tiger
that looked down from a tree.

There once was a terrible tiger
that came creeping after me.

There once was a terrible tiger
with teeth as sharp as sharp could be.

That terrible, terrible tiger –
will he eat **me**?

That terrible, terrible tiger,
he roared ... and leapt at me.

I cuddled that terrible tiger.
He's really my kitten, you see.